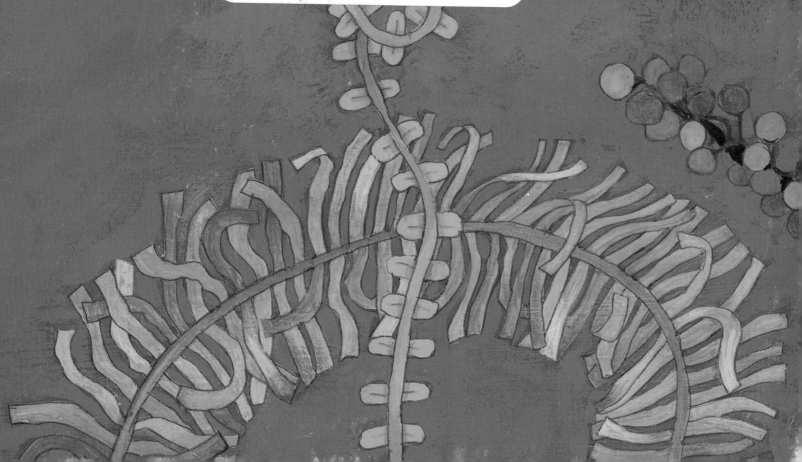

Also by David McKee:

Elmer and Rose
Elmer and Snake
Elmer and Super El
Elmer and the Big Bird
Elmer and the Birthday Quake
Elmer and the Hippos
Elmer and the Rainbow
Elmer and the Whales
Elmer's Christmas
Elmer's First Counting Book
Elmer's Opposites
Elmer's Special Day

for Princess Bakhta

American edition published in 2014 by Andersen Press USA, an imprint of Andersen Press Ltd.
www.andersenpressusa.com

Paperback edition published in 2012 by Andersen Press Ltd.
Published in Australia by Random House Australia Pty., Level 3, 100 Pacific Highway, North Sydney, NSW 2060.
First published in Great Britain in 2002 by Andersen Press Ltd.

Distributed in the United States and Canada by
Lerner Publishing Group, Inc.
241 First Avenue North
Minneapolis, MN 55401 USA
For reading levels and more information, look up this title at www.lernerbooks.com.
Color separated in Switzerland by Photolitho AG, Zürich.
Printed and bound in Malaysia by Tien Wah Press.
David McKee has used gouache in this book.

Library of Congress Cataloging-in-Publication data available.
ISBN: 978–1–4677–6326–4
eBook ISBN: 978–1–4677–6327–1
1 – TWP – 4/15/14

This book has been printed on acid-free paper

ELMER
and Butterfly

David McKee

Andersen Press USA

Elmer, the patchwork elephant, was out walking
when a shout came from up a tree: "Hello, Elmer."
"Is that you, Monkey?" Elmer called back.
"No, it's me," laughed cousin Wilbur from behind
a bush.
"Hello, Wilbur," chuckled Elmer. "You are clever
with your voice tricks. I'm going for a walk.
See you later."

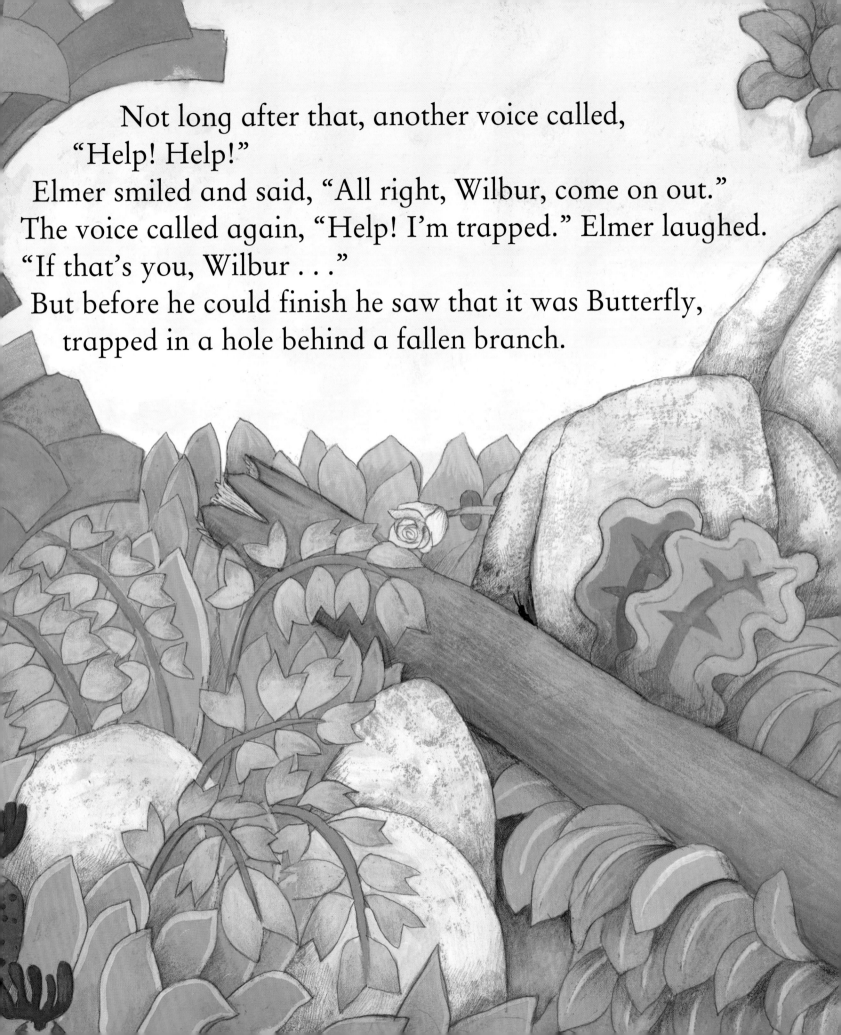

Not long after that, another voice called,
"Help! Help!"
Elmer smiled and said, "All right, Wilbur, come on out."
The voice called again, "Help! I'm trapped." Elmer laughed.
"If that's you, Wilbur . . ."
But before he could finish he saw that it was Butterfly,
trapped in a hole behind a fallen branch.

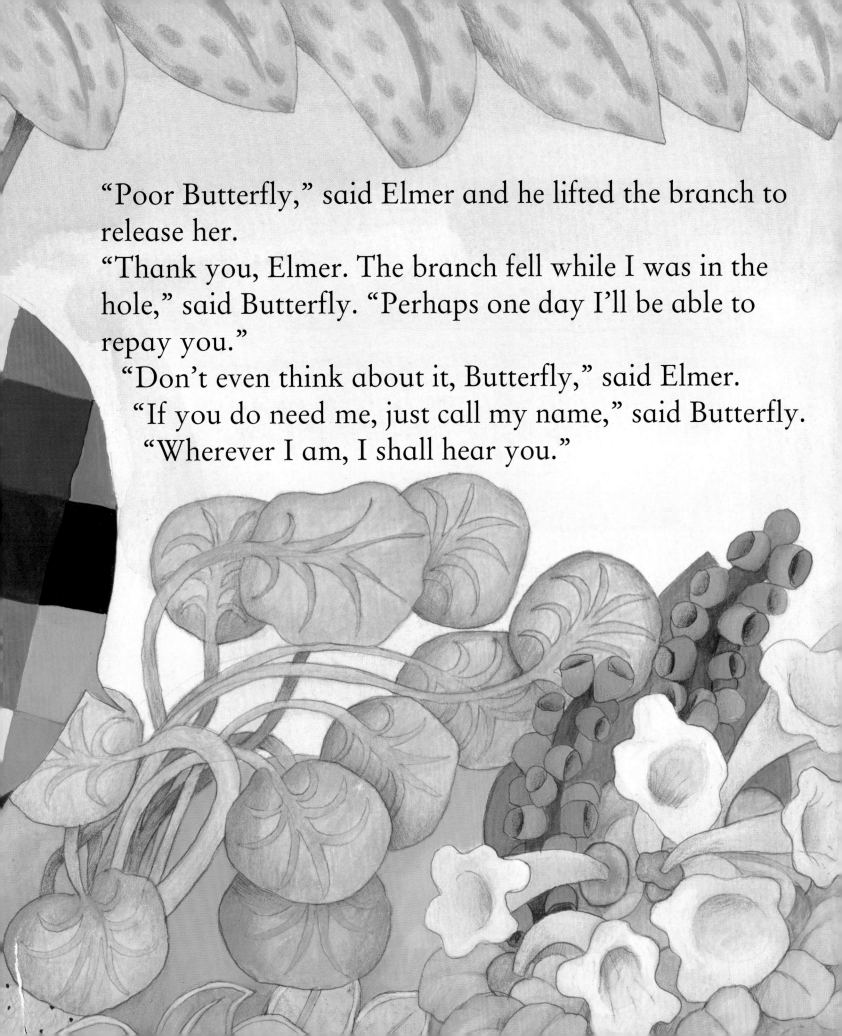

"Poor Butterfly," said Elmer and he lifted the branch to release her.

"Thank you, Elmer. The branch fell while I was in the hole," said Butterfly. "Perhaps one day I'll be able to repay you."

"Don't even think about it, Butterfly," said Elmer.

"If you do need me, just call my name," said Butterfly. "Wherever I am, I shall hear you."

"A butterfly saving an elephant, that's a good one!"
chuckled Elmer as he continued his walk.
At that point, a narrow path led off the main one.
"I've never been here before," he said.
"This looks interesting."

The path suddenly led out of the trees and along a cliff high above the valley below.

"This is dangerous," said Elmer. "And the path goes to a cave. I'll go back . . . Oh, dear! Going backwards here isn't easy. I'll go to the cave, turn around and walk back normally."

Elmer was nearly there when the path started falling.
He rushed into the cave and peeked out. Part of the
path had gone.
"Oh no! There's no way back," he said. "Help!"
he shouted. There was no answer.

"Help!" Elmer called again. Still no answer.
"They're all too far away," he thought. "I'll try Butterfly.
Butterfly! Help!" he called.
He was about to try again when Butterfly arrived.

"Oh, Butterfly, thank goodness!" said Elmer.
"Now it's me who is trapped in a hole."
"Don't worry, Elmer," said Butterfly.
"I'll get help."

Wilbur was amusing a group of elephants when Butterfly arrived. She quickly told them about Elmer. In no time the elephants were rushing to the rescue.

At the cliff top the elephants saw how dangerous it was and most kept away from the edge. Wilbur disappeared back among the trees.

One or two elephants carefully peeked over the edge to try and spot Elmer. "I see his trunk," said one.

Wilbur soon came hurrying back, pulling
a very long, very strong vine.
He threw one end over the edge of the cliff
and called down, "Grab it, Elmer."

"Tie the vine around you and hold on tightly," said Butterfly. "Don't worry. It will be all right."

Elmer tied the vine firmly and called out, "I'm ready."
The elephants grabbed the vine and pulled. Elmer swung out from the cave and then upwards.

Once he was safe, Elmer thanked them all,
especially Butterfly.
"Fancy a butterfly saving an elephant!" he said.
Then a shout came from the cave, "Don't forget me."
The elephants stared. "Who else is there?" said one.
"Just Wilbur's voice," laughed Elmer. "Let's tickle him."
But Wilbur was already running home.